Mango Trees

Written by Tae-yeon Kim
Illustrated by Gu-seon Muhn
Edited by Joy Cowley

big&SMALL

What if there were no mango trees
growing in the Philippines?

Mangoes grow in tropical and subtropical regions. The Philippines is famous for its sweet mangoes.

Philippine mangoes are famous.
Yellow mangoes are ripe and sweet.
Green mangoes are sour and are used
to give sourness to savory dishes.
Once you have tasted mango,
you will never forget the flavor.
People buy baskets of dried mango
to eat when it is not mango season.
If there were no mango trees
in the Philippines, the people could not
enjoy such delicious flavors.

What if there were no narra trees
growing in the Philippines?

The wood of the narra tree
is used to make furniture
and statues of Bulol, the god of rice.
Rice farmers believe Bulol protects
their harvest. If there were no narra trees
in the Philippines, the rice farmers
would not have Bulol statues to help them.

 Step-like rice fields in Banaue, known as the "Rice Terraces of the Philippine Cordilleras", are a World Heritage site. These terraces were made by the local indigenous Ifugao tribe, on the sides of mountains.

What if there were no bamboo trees growing in the Philippines?

Bamboo is good for building houses.
Bamboo houses are cool in hot weather
because the breeze can pass through them.
And, if there were no bamboo trees,
there would be no beautiful music
inside this Philippine church.

This 180-year-old bamboo organ sounds like the voice of an angel. It would not exist if there was no bamboo in the Philippines.

What if there were no coconut palms growing in the Philippines?

The juice from coconuts can be
drunk and the flesh can be eaten.
The fruit of coconut palms
is sold to other countries.
Filipinos consider the coconut palm
as the tree of life.

Filipino is the Spanish word for people from the Philippines.
The Philippines was once a colony of Spain.

If there were no coconut palm trees
growing in the Philippines,
the people would not have many things.

What is one of the most important fruits?
It is the coconut!

From coconuts, people make soft drinks,
cookies, sweets, soap and cosmetics.
Dried coconut is used for baking.
Coconut oil is used for ointments
and coconut fiber is used for mats.

The oil squeezed out of coconuts is used in cooking and cosmetics.

What if there were no mangrove trees growing in the Philippines?

At a glance, mangrove trees
seem to be floating on water.
They put their roots down deep
through salty water, to the mud.
Do you know why mangrove trees
are so important?

The roots, breathing under water,
make the sea clean and protect
small fish and other sea creatures.
The trees protect the coastline
from waves that surge in storms.

23

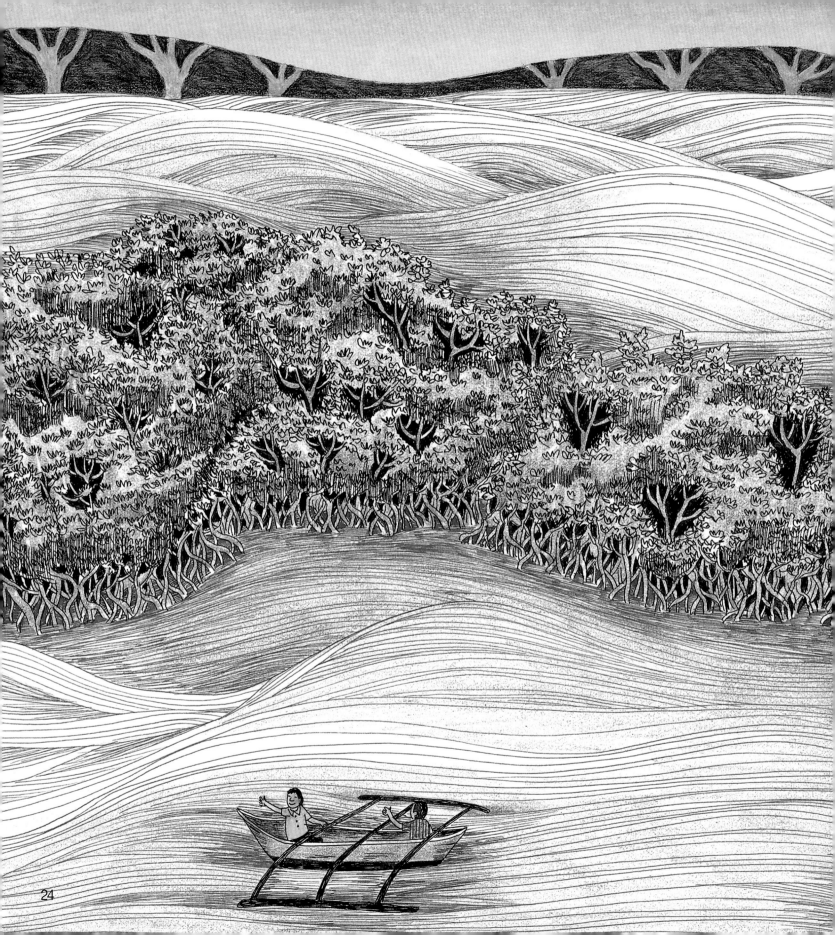

If there were no mangrove trees
growing in the Philippines, the people would
not have such a beautiful coast.

About the Philippines
Country of Simplicity and Nature

The national flag of the Philippines includes red which stands for courage and blue which represents peace and justice. The white triangle is for equality, while the yellow sun in the triangle stands for unity and freedom. The three stars represent the three main islands: Luzon, Panay and Mindanao.

The Queen of Trees

The narra is the national tree of the Philippines. Philippine people often call the narra tree the "queen of trees." Furniture and floors made from narra wood can last a long time. Because it can endure many hardships, the narra represents its country.

In the Philippines there are many places where narra trees are planted and grown for timber.

Manila Cathedral, First Built with Trees

Philippine people use bamboo to build traditional houses and the leaves of nipa palm trees to thatch the roofs. Even Manila Cathedral, the Philippines' oldest cathedral, was first built with trees. A succession of earthquakes and wars means that it has been repeatedly rebuilt. Manila Cathedral was most recently rebuilt in 1958. The Philippines is the only Asian nation where Catholocism is the official national religion. This is because Spain, a Catholic nation, colonized the Philippines a long time ago.

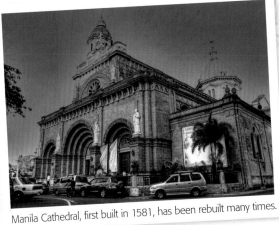

Manila Cathedral, first built in 1581, has been rebuilt many times.

What Is Bamboo in the Philippine Language?

Filipinos call bamboo "kawayan." This is in their Tagalog language. Filipinos use both English and Tagalog together. Tagalog is the language of the indigenous community. One third of the population speak it.

Morning

Afternoon

Night

 English and Tagalog have varying greetings at different times of the day.

The Island Nation

An island nation is a country surrounded by sea. The Philippines is located in the South West Pacific and is made up of over 7,000 small and large islands. Most of these islands were created by volcanic activity. Underwater eruptions of lava have piled up to build many of these islands. It is believed that millions of years ago others were split from the Asian continental shelf by volcanic activity.

Taal Volcano that has been raised up in a lake

Many Different People Living on the Different Islands

Not all of the over 7,000 islands are populated: less than one thousand are inhabited by people. The capital city, Manila, is on Luzon Island, the largest in the Philippines. The area which is now the Philippines was originally inhabited by many different tribal groups that were strongly influenced by Malay culture. After occupations by Spain and the United States, there is now a strong influence from these cultures too.

Tasty Bananas

You can see banana trees everywhere in the Philippines. People eat bananas in many ways. They fry them on sticks, or mix them with spices.

Banana Cue

Put a stick through a banana and fry it in hot oil.

Turon

Wrap half a banana in rice paper and then bake it.

Suman

Wrap a rice cake in a banana leaf and steam it.

Philippine People Love Animals

In the Bohol islands there is a special sanctuary for tarsiers. They are small animals with enormous eyes. Their bodies are only 4–6 inches in size, smaller than an adult's hand, but they have long tails which help them climb trees.

A tarsier is smaller than an adult's hand.

In the sea near Donsol there are many whale sharks.

In the Donsol region, there are whale sharks. Although large, whale sharks are calm and docile.

The Philippines' national bird is the Philippine eagle. It is the world's largest eagle. But the destruction of forests has reduced the number of these birds. People now raise these eagles in captivity to help increase their numbers. The first bird born in captivity was called Pag-asa, meaning "hope" in Tagalog.

The Philippine eagle is endangered.

Philippines

Name: Republic of the Philippines

Location: Southeast Asia

Area: 120,000 mi² (300,000 km²)

Capital: Manila

Population: 96,710,000 (2012)

Language: Tagalog, English

Religion: Catholic (Christianity)

Main exports: Electronics, copper, coconut products, clothing, bananas, furniture, gold, wood

South China Sea

Philippine Sea

Vigan

Luzon Island

*Rice Terraces
Made by the Ifugao tribe
in the Philippines

*Bangka Boat
Traditional Filipino fishing boat

*Philippines

Manila

*Narra Tree
The national tree of the Philippines

*Taal Volcano
Located in a lake, the beautiful
Taal Volcano is one of many active
volcanos in the Philippines.

Donsol

Roxas

Panay Island

Tacloban

Cebu

Palawan Island

Bohol
Island

Puerto Princesa

Butuan

*Jeepney
The most popular form of public
transport in the Philippines

Iligan

Mindanao Island

Original Korean text by Tae-yeon Kim
Illustrations by Gu-seon Muhn
Korean edition © Aram Publishing

This English edition published by big & SMALL in 2015
by arrangement with Aram Publishing
English text edited by Joy Cowley
English edition © big & SMALL 2015

Distributed in the United States and Canada by
Lerner Publishing Group, Inc.
241 First Avenue North
Minneapolis, MN 55401 U.S.A.
www.lernerbooks.com

Photo attributions by page no. - left to right, top to bottom
Page 26: public domain; Page 27: © Kuranges (CC-BY-SA-3.0);
Page 28: public domain; public domain; public domain; public domain;
Page 29: "Tarsius syrichta" © Plerzelwupp (CC-BY-SA-3.0); public domain;
© Rusty Ferguson (Cebuexperience.com) (CC-BY-2.0)

All rights reserved

ISBN: 978-1-925233-46-9

Printed in Korea